To anyone who ever felt like they didn't fit in,
this book is for you.

Every child deserves to shine.

To Peter and my girls, thank you for your love and

remarkable patience.

It is important to note that this book is a work of fiction, and it should not in any way be used as a diagnosis for dyspraxia. There are many varying symptoms and variances of the condition, and whilst I hope this book brings awareness, it is important to seek professional guidance and support if you would like further information or advice.

PRIYA
A PANDA WITH DYSPRAXIA

Written by Jo North
Illustrated by Robert Hooper

Priya smiled at her mum as they ate breakfast, but her mum could see she was looking worried.

"What's the matter? Aren't you excited to see your friends and show them your new presents?" her mum asked. It had been Priya's birthday yesterday, and she had been given a new coat, a pair of trainers and some pens and pencils.

Priya couldn't wait to show her friends her new coat (it was bright blue which was her favourite colour!), but she felt embarrassed at what her friends would think of her other gifts.

She loved that her trainers lit up when she ran, but instead of laces they had Velcro. Most of her friends had laces on their trainers now, and she didn't want them to laugh at her.

Her new pencils had special grips on them which would make writing easier for her, but Priya was worried because none of her friends had pencils like that.

Her mum seemed to know what she was thinking, and gave her a cuddle. "Priya, your presents are going to help you so much in school and make everything much easier for you. I'm sure your friends are going to love them."

Priya had recently been diagnosed with a condition called dyspraxia, which meant she sometimes found it difficult to get her body to do what she wanted it to. She knew exactly how to tie up shoelaces and use buttons, but she just found them so difficult to actually do.

Her dyspraxia also meant she found writing really hard as trying to hold her pen and make it move in the way she wanted just didn't seem to work.

It was so frustrating!

In many ways, Priya felt quite relieved when the doctor explained about dyspraxia. She had always thought she was just really clumsy, and didn't understand why nobody else found these tasks difficult!

Her mum had never heard of dyspraxia either so together they read lots about it and spoke to Priya's teacher about what they could do to help her at school.

Priya's class had art for their first lesson, and they had to make posters for the Christmas fair next week. Priya nervously took out her new pencils, but nobody even noticed them!

She found they really did make the task much easier, and she was very pleased with her poster. Her friend Emma even said how brilliant it looked when she walked past, which made Priya very happy!

Later that day when they were getting ready for PE, Mr Lewis set them all a challenge to find some cones he had hidden in the playground. Priya and her friends giggled as they rushed to get their trainers on.

As Priya did her trainers up, she felt so relieved that she didn't have laces – she knew she would have been the last one out of the changing room if she did.

Priya grinned happily as she spotted one of the hidden cones, and ran to collect it.

"Wow, I love your trainers – look at the way they flash!" Dylan shouted over to Priya, as he found another hidden cone under the slide.

She smiled and thanked him, and thought about what her mum had said that morning. Her presents really had helped her today, and she had not felt worried or embarrassed at all. She thought about her dyspraxia and realised that with a few small changes, it didn't need to stop her from doing anything she wanted!

At the end of the lesson, Priya ran over to join her friends, who were chatting about the fact it was Christmas in a few weeks' time.

"I wonder what presents we'll get!" said Dylan excitedly.

"I don't know" replied Priya, jumping in the air so her trainers flashed again, "but I can't wait to find out!"

The End

10% of all book sales will go to a charity for dyspraxia. To learn more about Shine Books and the author Jo North, please visit www.shine-books.com

SHINE

More titles in the Shine series:

- ★ Dylan, a dog with dyslexia
- ★ Alice, an aardvark with autism
- ★ Emma, an elephant with epilepsy
- ★ Ollie, an otter with OCD
- ★ Charlie, a chimpanzee with ADHD